MAX

VIKING ADVENTURE

BY SAMANTHA METCALF

ILLUSTRATED BY IAN R. WARD

First published in Great Britain in 2017 by:
Mysteries in Time Limited
www.mysteriesintime.com

Reprinted 2021

Illustrated by Ian R. Ward
www.ianrward.co.uk

A catalogue record for this book is available from the British Library.

ISBN 978-0-9935660-8-0

Hi! I'm Katie and I am 8 years old. Max is my older brother. He's really clever. He helps me with my home work when I'm stuck. He knows everything! But don't tell him I said that. He can get really annoying and know-it-all. He is always telling me stuff, but sometimes it's just too much. All I want is a simple answer, like 'yes' or 'no'. Instead, it's always 'maybe, because...' So annoying.

But he's not so bad. He always looks out for me. And we have fun playing games together.

I think my favourite thing is playing outside in any weather! I love going to the park, especially the adventure playground with the huge, curly slide. You can go really fast on that one, especially when you lie down! Mum hates it when I come home covered in mud, but I can't help it. The fun parts of the park are always the muddiest.

Hey, I'm Max and I'm 11. I love reading. I read comics and cartoons that make me laugh, and I read adventure stories about knights and castles, or pirates and buried treasure! Mum is always telling me I have an over-active imagination. I can't help it. My mind just starts picturing loads of weird stuff.

I also love solving puzzles. Grandpa always buys me books full of word-searches and crosswords. I like to time myself and see how fast I can solve them.

Katie is my younger sister. She is really energetic and fun to be around. She's really fast and sporty. I wish I could be as good as her at sports. But don't tell her I said that. She can also be really annoying, when she can't sit still for more than five minutes. And she doesn't stop talking!

But she's cool. I'm pleased she's my sister.

1

BEEP BEEP BEEP!

The red light on the metal detector was flashing along with the constant sound of the buzzer.

It was a bright spring afternoon and Max and Katie were in Grandpa's back garden using his metal detector.

They were looking for buried treasure.

There had been a buzz across the whole town ever since a local farmer had found an ancient hoard of Viking treasure in one of his fields last week. Everyone was excited about what could be beneath their feet.

"There could be hundreds of years' history right here!" shrieked Max.

"More importantly, we could find buried treasure and we'll be rich!" exclaimed Katie. "The newspapers will print our pictures, we'll be interviewed on

TV and the Queen will want to meet us. We'll be famous!"

Max had laughed as his sister got carried away in her daydream. It WAS exciting.

Suddenly there was a noise. They all stopped.

The metal detector was beeping. This could only mean one thing: they had found something.

2

Grandpa caught the metal detector that Katie had now pushed aside before it fell to the ground with a crash. Katie hadn't even noticed; she was already digging.

Katie shrieked as her fingers closed around something solid. Max helped her dig deeper and brush the soil from the small buried object.

"What have you found?" asked Grandpa.

Max and Katie were both frowning seriously at their small treasure.

Max cleaned it in a bucket of water and held it up.

"Is it an ancient brooch?" asked Katie. "Or an old coin? Or part of a Viking weapon? Or a button from a lady's beautiful dress?"

Max turned it in the light. He had no answer.

Grandpa moved the newspaper from the garden

chair and sat down. Max placed the treasure in Grandpa's up-turned palm.

Grandpa leaned in closer and squinted through his glasses.

"Wonderful!" he exclaimed, slapping his leg in happiness.

Max and Katie looked at him.

"Do you know what this is?" asked Max.

"Yes!" he laughed. "It's an old medal. You can see its shape has been worn down over time. Look, you can just see the colours here."

Grandpa was pointing to a faint shade of red on one side.

"How do you know it's a medal?" asked Katie. "How old do you think it is?"

Grandpa smiled. "This medal dates from the Second World War. I know this, because it belonged to my uncle. It was very important to him. I loved playing with it when I was a child, many years ago. I lost it one day and got into terrible trouble. And now you've found it! Thank you very much."

Grandpa hugged them both.

Max and Katie were a little disappointed that they hadn't found some ancient treasure. But it was better than treasure for Grandpa. It was memories.

3

Back home, Max and Katie found their very own treasure: a turquoise box was waiting for them on the kitchen table. It was time for a new adventure.

They raced upstairs and opened the box.

They found the Mission Plan.

Max's eyes lit up when he saw their new destination.

"You'll never guess where we're going this time!" he challenged Katie.

"You know I'm rubbish at guessing games," moaned Katie. "Just tell me!"

"We're going on a Viking adventure!" grinned Max.

Katie clapped her hands in delight. "I've always wanted to wear a helmet with horns!"

She then settled down to listen to their latest mission.

Mission Plan

Place: Viking Danelaw
Date: AD 887

A Viking ship returned from a raid on a
monastery, but all the sailors on board were
very ill. The only person who was not sick was
the kidnapped monk from the monastery. The
villagers were suspicious of this stranger.
Had he poisoned them? Cast a spell on them?
Cursed them?

The villagers decided they should fight back
by raiding more monasteries as well as nearby
Anglo-Saxon villages. Their revenge started a
long and bloody war.

Task:

Can you help keep the peace between the newly-
settled Vikings and the Anglo-Saxons?

4

"Who were the Anglo-Saxons?" asked Katie.

Max picked up the history magazine to find the answer.

"Before the Vikings came to England, the Anglo-Saxons were the people living here," explained Max.

"Why did the Vikings attack monasteries?" asked Katie. "It seems a bit unfair to attack a church, which wouldn't have been protected or guarded."

"Most Anglo-Saxons were Christian, whereas the Vikings were Pagans and worshipped several gods," explained Max. "There were many monasteries across the country, where monks lived peacefully. These monasteries were full of golden crosses, cups and other religious items, which attracted the Vikings. They were easy targets for the Viking warriors."

"Sounds like the Vikings were greedy!" replied Katie. "Where is this place that we're going to...

Danelaw?"

"The Anglo-Saxons and the Vikings kept fighting," explained Max. "So they made a deal. Borders were agreed and the Vikings were given an area of England where they could settle and live peacefully. They called this area 'Danelaw'."

Max and Katie read on and learnt about how the Vikings travelled far and wide. "Look!" exclaimed Max. "The Vikings even beat Christopher Columbus to reach North America first!"

They learnt about the Viking longships and how their design meant they could travel along shallow rivers or even sail straight onto beaches to attack quickly.

Katie was disappointed when she realised that Vikings did not wear horned helmets. She threw down the history magazine and kept shaking her head.

"What?!" she shrieked. "But why do cartoons

always show Vikings wearing helmets with horns if it's a myth?!"

Max laughed. He agreed. It was funny that everyone believed something that might not be true.

"Talking about clothes, I think we need to visit Grandpa's shop."

5

Max and Katie waved goodbye to Mum, who watched them walk along the path towards Grandpa's fancy dress shop.

"Hi Grandpa," smiled Katie when they arrived. "We have decided to learn more about the Vikings now that we know they used to live around here."

Max was amazed at how easily Katie lied. She was an expert. He would have stuttered and started to sweat. He would have looked guilty before he'd even opened his mouth.

As they followed Grandpa to the back of the shop, where the Viking costumes were kept, Max whispered to his sister.

"Psst," he hissed. "How do you lie so easily?!"

Katie looked offended. She stopped and turned to him. "But I didn't lie," she said. "We DO want to learn more about the Vikings. It's completely true. I just didn't explain HOW we're going to learn more about the Vikings."

She turned with a triumphant flick of her hair, and marched off after Grandpa.

Max realised she was absolutely right. She was actually being completely truthful. He smiled to himself and caught up with them.

Grandpa had already picked a costume for them both. Max's tunic was brown with maroon trousers.

Katie's dress was long and blue, worn over a cream tunic. The dress fastened at the front using two pretty brooches with strings of colourful beads hanging between them.

"I love it!" she squealed. "So much better than a helmet with horns."

She added a white cloth to cover her hair and they both admired their reflections.

"Thanks Grandpa!" they both called out as they left the shop.

It was time to travel through history.

6

Safely back in Max's bedroom, Max gently closed the door so Mum wouldn't hear them. They had shown their costumes to her after they returned home, explaining that Grandpa had helped choose them. Max could see that Mum thought they were adorable, which annoyed him a lot.

Max gave Katie the Time Travel Sticker, which was a blue pattern within an outline that reminded Katie of an anchor.

"This is Thor's hammer," explained Max. "It was considered a lucky symbol by the Vikings."

"Thor!" squealed Katie in delight. "I know who Thor is! He's a Viking god, who makes thunder and lightning with his mighty hammer."

Max smiled. This was an exciting adventure. They had both heard so much about the Vikings already.

Katie was busy admiring the pretty pattern of the Time Travel Sticker and had to be reminded to put it on.

They were ready. Max programmed the time machine for AD 887 and Katie pushed the red button on top of the time machine.

7

The glass beads that decorated Katie's dress were rattling together tunefully as the energy of time travel transported them back through history.

They felt soft ground beneath their feet and looked around. There was a thick fog surrounding them, which meant they couldn't get their bearings. Where were they?

There was an eerie silence that made Max worry that he had programmed the time machine with the wrong date or place.

Max and Katie stood very, very still. Listening. There was a faint sound. What was it? It sounded like water, like slight ripples on a calm surface.

Just as they strained their ears towards the sound, a dark shadow grew from the mist and towered above them. The closer it got, the clearer the shape became.

It was some sort of creature with a frightening face looming over them. It was just an outline, a silhouette.

Max's blood went cold.

It looked like a dragon.

8

Max and Katie huddled together in fear. Max couldn't take his eyes off the menacing shape, when a gust of wind cleared a patch of mist.

Suddenly, the scene started to make sense. The dragon's head was made from wood: it was the carved front of a Viking ship. There was a river that passed in front of where Max and Katie were standing, which explained the sounds they had heard. There were several brightly-painted shields attached to the side of the ship. The large square sail was opened fully, but there was barely a breeze.

Max also realised that they weren't alone in watching this ship glide past. There were several people no longer wrapped in the ghostly mist.

Max and Katie watched as two young men on the riverside threw rope around the neck of the dragon. They pulled with all their strength, until the ship was brought to a stop.

Everyone waited.

Silence.

"Hello?" called one of the men with the rope.

The sound was muffled in the mist.

Everyone held their breath as they strained to hear if anyone on board replied. Katie thought she heard a distant mumbling, but couldn't be sure.

"This is very strange," said a young Viking next to Max. "A Viking ship is known for its noisy homecoming."

"Do you recognise this ship?" asked Max, wondering whether perhaps it was an ambush.

"Yes, this is the ship of our strongest warriors," replied the young Viking. "I'm Eirik. You must be from another village?"

Max nodded. "Er, yes, we are from a village very far away. I'm Max and this is my sister, Katie."

After their introductions, they all watched as a

few people stepped up onto the ship to investigate. They quickly called out to the people on the ground to help.

Max and Katie climbed onto the ship using the rope to pull themselves up, reminding Max of PE classes at school. He wasn't very good at it, but Katie pulled herself up effortlessly.

Once they were on the ship, they looked around.

There were people lying everywhere using animal skins as blankets to keep themselves warm. Many of them were sleeping, some looked as though they were dreaming with their eyes open, trembling and groaning in pain.

"What's happened to them?" asked Katie. "I thought Vikings were meant to be strong and loud!"

Max looked from man to man. There was only one man on the whole ship who did not look ill. Instead, he looked worried. His hands were tied and he wore a necklace with a cross around his neck.

"That must be the monk that the Vikings kidnapped," whispered Max. "He's the only one who isn't ill."

There was one Viking who was less weak than the others. He was holding a selection of stones in his hand and trying to speak.

Max looked closely at the stones. He could see a symbol carved onto each stone.

"What are those symbols?" asked Katie.

"They are Runes," replied Max quietly. "They are the letters of the Viking alphabet."

"So why is that man showing them to us?" Katie pointed to the man's outstretched palm. "Is he trying to spell something out?"

Katie leaned closer to the man.

"What's your name?" she asked gently.

"Sigurd," he replied.

Eirik looked closely at the Runes, then gasped and stumbled back.

"What is it?" asked Max.

"Those Runes," started Eirik. "They say there is a curse on this ship. We are all in danger."

9

"What kind of danger?" asked Katie.

Eirik looked at her with a serious expression.

"I don't know," he said, looking towards the monk. "Perhaps we need to speak to the prisoner to find out."

Max and Katie followed him to the back of the ship, where the monk was waiting with wide, anxious eyes.

"Tell us what happened here," demanded Eirik.

The monk looked at each of them in turn. He opened and closed his mouth, trying to speak, but his throat was dry.

Eirik had a flask of water tied to his belt, which he gently tipped to the monk's lips and poured. The monk drank so fast that he coughed before trying to speak again.

"Thank you, thank you," he repeated. "I haven't

had a drink since we left my monastery early this morning."

The monk looked around at the sick men on the ship and started to tell the story from the beginning.

"I was praying early this morning at first light, when I heard the door bang open. Suddenly, the church filled with these bearded giants!" he waved his hand towards the sick men on the ship. "They

were wearing animal skins round their shoulders and thrusting axes and swords in the air."

"It must have been a terrifying sight," said Katie.

"It was. I had heard of these fierce warriors from across the seas before, but I never imagined they would attack my little church by the coast. We live a peaceful life away from the politics of the land."

"What happened when they arrived?" asked Max.

"They took everything they could carry!" exclaimed the monk. "They filled a large wooden chest with anything made of metal, especially if it was silver or gold. They even took the sacred cross from the wall. And then they took me."

Katie was confused. "But why didn't they take your necklace?"

The monk looked down and smiled. "This? This is carved from wood. It's worthless to them. They can't melt it down into weapons or trade it in foreign lands."

Max was quiet for a moment.

"All this happened early this morning, which means the sickness started after you were taken prisoner," he said.

The monk nodded. "Yes, everyone was definitely strong and well when they attacked my monastery."

"Then what caused everyone except you to fall ill?" asked Eirik suspiciously. "Why didn't you also fall sick?"

The monk realised it looked suspicious. He started to sweat. He shook his head desperately.

"I don't know!" he cried out. "I have no answer! Everyone started to turn pale and collapse. But I promise there is no such curse as that man over there claims."

Everyone looked back to Sigurd, the man clutching the Rune stones.

Sigurd was watching them all like a hawk.

10

"Don't listen to him!" cried Sigurd angrily. "As soon as we left his monastery, we started to fall sick. The people who touched the treasure were the first to get ill."

Max looked around at the various sacks and wooden chests dotted around the ship.

"Where is the stolen hoard?" he asked.

Sigurd laughed. "What? You think we would keep such a cursed treasure with us?" He paused to cough. "No, we didn't want to bring the same fate on the village. We buried it all beneath the ancient oak tree where the river splits into two. We had to protect the village!"

There was no time to talk any further, because it was time to help get the weak patients off the ship. Everyone nearby gave a helping hand. The giant Vikings were stooped over in pain, so they seemed less frightening than the monk's description. They were still heavy though, and it took two strong men to help each one off the ship. Max and Katie helped the monk onto dry land, then walked with him in the procession back to the village.

"What are your names?" he asked on the way.

Max introduced himself and Katie.

"Nice to meet you," said Katie. "What's your name?"

"I'm Father Godwin," he replied.

They continued to walk the rest of the journey in friendly silence, each thinking about what was waiting for them ahead.

11

The mist was almost clear by the time they arrived at the village. There was a central longhouse with a thatched roof held up with logs. There was smoke rising up from a gap in the roof and pleasant cooking smells drifted in the breeze. There were many smaller houses nearby.

There were sheep and goats grazing and Katie was excited to see a few lambs too. Max watched the blacksmiths carefully as they hit glowing red-hot metal with a hammer to mould it into a new shape.

They were led through the village and as the skies cleared, Max and Katie were amazed to see a grand castle emerge from the mist.

Max, Katie and the monk followed Eirik and the other Vikings through the castle gates. They were led into a throne room by castle guards, where everyone fell silent as a tall man wearing a crown stepped forward.

Katie gasped. "Is that the king?!" she whispered.

Eirik nodded. "He's the King of The Danelaw."

Katie clapped her hands in delight, then felt her cheeks grow hot as she realised everyone was looking at her.

The king signalled to his guards, who pushed Father Godwin forward and forced him to kneel before the king.

The king looked down at the monk with angry

eyes. "So you are the devil who has cursed our men."

Father Godwin looked up.

"No, your majesty!" he started. "I have not put any curse on your men! I do not know any such curse or spell. I am a monk, not a wizard. I wish no ill harm to any of your people. I live a simple life by the sea and hope to return to my monastery soon to continue living peacefully."

The crowd started to jeer and shout at the monk.

"Don't trust him!" shouted one.

"He's lying!" called another.

"We need to retaliate and get revenge!" called a third voice.

The king signalled to the guards to take the monk to the cells while he decided what to do.

"We cannot be seen to be weak," he announced. "I will start to plan our next move."

Max and Katie looked at each other. This could start a terrible war. They had to do something.

12

Outside, Max and Katie were grateful for the fresh air. Eirik joined them and they found a quiet place to talk.

"We cannot let them start a war," said Eirik. "There will be terrible consequences. Hundreds of innocent people will die."

Max nodded. "I agree. We need to find out what caused this mysterious sickness."

"But how?!" exclaimed Katie, throwing her hands in the air. "The only evidence is the buried treasure, but we'll never find that!"

Eirik raised a hand. "That's not true. We know it was buried beneath the large oak tree where the river divides. It's not far. I can take you there."

"Let's go," said Max. "We don't have much time."

Eirik led them down to the river's edge, where there was a small rowing boat lying upside down.

Max and Katie helped Eirik turn it over and lift it into the water. They all climbed in and Eirik started rowing back along the river in the direction that the Viking ship had come from.

They rowed for about an hour, until the river split in two directions.

"We're here," announced Eirik.

They jumped onto the soft grass and pulled the boat out of the water. It didn't take long to work out where to dig; the only tree in this area was a large oak tree with a thick trunk. When they got closer, they saw that the ground to one side was disturbed. This was the spot.

"Are you sure you want to do this?" asked Eirik. "What if that treasure really is cursed?"

Katie laughed. "There's no such thing as a curse!"

Eirik smiled too. "We hope not."

They started to dig.

It didn't take long before they reached something

solid. They brushed the soil from around it with their bare hands and pulled out a large wooden chest.

"Here goes!" said Max. "We need to prove that this treasure can't make people sick."

Max opened the chest and stepped back with shock.

It was empty.

13

"This makes no sense!" exclaimed Max. "There is no way anyone else had time to get here before us!"

Eirik was thinking. "You're right," he said. "There is only one explanation: the chest was empty when it was buried."

"Why on earth would anyone bury an empty chest?" laughed Katie.

"They wanted everyone else on that ship to believe they were burying the cursed treasure," explained Max. "But they had already stolen it and hidden it somewhere."

"So there was never any curse, just an elaborate plot to steal some gold?" asked Katie.

"Exactly."

"But it's had terrible consequences," she continued. "The king is about to go to war for no reason!"

14

Max and Katie carried the empty chest to the boat, which Eirik pushed into the water. They rowed back to the village as quickly as they could. They had to find the missing treasure before it was too late.

Along the way they came up with a plan.

"The thief has to be someone who was on that ship," said Max.

"Yes," agreed Eirik. "Nothing was carried off the ship except the people on board, all belongings were left behind. The whole ship was put into quarantine, in case anything else was cursed."

"What do you mean?" asked Katie.

"To stop anyone else from falling sick, nobody will be allowed back on that ship," explained Max. "The king will have put guards there to stop anyone from getting on and taking anything."

Katie's eyes widened. "That means the treasure

must still be on the ship!"

They rowed up alongside the ship and pulled the little boat up onto the river bank. They approached the two guards to explain what they had found. The guards did not look interested in anything they had to say.

Katie realised they had to be creative.

"Do you know what this is?" she asked, picking up the chest.

The two guards flicked their eyes briefly to the wooden chest, but only for a second.

"This is the chest that was buried with the cursed treasure. Anyone who comes into contact with it falls ill."

Katie stepped towards the guards and opened the chest slowly. The guards backed away slowly, until their backs were against the ship itself.

"Er, get that away from me!" cried one guard.

Katie stepped even closer.

"It's a terrible sickness," said Katie sadly. "Victims fall ill immediately and are too weak to stand by themselves. They are exhausted and drift in and out of a restless sleep."

"OK, you win!" said the second guard. "You can get onto the ship, just keep any of your wicked spells or curses away from us!"

Katie snapped the chest shut and skipped towards the ship. Max and Eirik grinned at her as they helped each other up onto the deck.

There were several barrels and bags dotted around the deck. They wasted no time and got to work searching the ship.

Most bags contained clothes or some dried food. But after searching for about twenty minutes, Katie's fingers closed around something cold and solid.

She pulled it out from the bag and gasped at the sight. It was a beautiful gold cross decorated with large rubies. Katie was mesmerised by the colours as the jewels caught the afternoon sunshine.

They emptied all the treasure from the bag and replaced it inside the wooden chest.

"We have found the treasure, but that doesn't explain what caused everyone to fall sick," said Eirik.

"Everyone except Father Godwin," corrected Max.

They decided to continue their search to see if they could find out what had poisoned everyone.

Max had an idea. He lifted the lid on the large water barrel and peered inside. The water level was low enough to see that there was something inside. He tipped the barrel over and stepped clear of the river of water as it spread over the deck.

Inside the now-empty barrel was the root of a plant.

"Is that there to give the water some flavour?" asked Katie innocently.

Eirik shook his head. "This plant is poisonous. Someone wanted those men to fall sick."

15

They raced back to the castle, where they explained everything to the guards on the gate. It wasn't until they saw the treasure inside the chest that the guards believed their story.

They were led to the same large hall where they had stood earlier listening to the king and were told to wait.

The king entered the hall with a determined walk and listened to everything they had to say. Eirik explained that there was a thief on that ship. Max continued by telling the king about finding the treasure inside one of the sailors' bags. Katie finished off by showing the poisonous root that they had found inside the drinking water.

"So it can't have been Father Godwin after all," said Katie ."There is no way that he could have hidden that treasure or put this root inside the water barrel. His hands were tied the whole time!"

"He was very thirsty when we found him," added Max. "He hadn't been given a drink since he was taken prisoner, which explains why he wasn't sick. And the fact that he didn't fall ill helped frame him for casting a fake curse."

The king was quiet for a few moments, thinking.

"This is very interesting," he started. "Do you have any suspects?"

Eirik spoke carefully. "There has to be one person who was only pretending to be ill, who was able to pretend to bury the treasure, someone who quickly pointed the finger at Father Godwin."

"Yes?" prompted the king.

"The man on the ship who held the Rune stones," replied Eirik. "It had to be him. It had to be the man called Sigurd."

16

The king had summoned everyone from the ship who could walk.

The king's advisers had created a herbal remedy to battle the poison of the root that the men had drank. This was given to Eirik, who moved around the room giving a cup of this remedy to each sick warrior.

When he came to the man who had held the Rune stones, Eirik paused and looked to the king. The king's guards pushed the man to his knees.

"Sigurd, we have learnt about your cowardly actions," started the king. "I will be more kind to you if you are honest and confess."

The man on his knees looked worried. "I... I... I don't know what you're talking about!"

"You put the poisonous plant inside the water barrel so everyone on the ship would get sick. Then you started a rumour that the treasure was cursed so that everyone would blame the monk!"

Sigurd shook his head aggressively.

"No!" he shrieked. "I found those Runes like that. I just picked them up. Please, you have to believe me!"

The king ignored his pleas. "You then stole the treasure and pretended to bury it, the whole time pretending to be sick yourself."

There was a collective gasp from the crowd as the king, whose voice was getting louder and louder, finished his accusations.

Sigurd was on his knees begging for his freedom.

"I promise you, I am innocent!" he cried. "I did not do any of these things. I looked less ill than the others because I WAS less ill! I must have drunk less water. Simple as that! I'm telling the truth."

The king shook his head. "The evidence all points to you. You had already hidden the gold, so you only pretended to bury the treasure. You buried an empty chest."

"But... But... But I didn't bury the treasure," he shrieked. "I was too sick to leave the ship!"

The king frowned at Sigurd. "If you didn't bury the chest, then who did?"

17

"It was Olav!" he cried, looking around desperately, hoping to find him in the crowd.

The crowd murmured and stepped away from one man, who was left standing on his own. The crowd had pointed out Olav, who was starting to sweat. He started to back away from the king, looking for an exit. The guards were too quick for him; he was surrounded in no time.

The king looked at this new traitor.

"Why?" he asked simply.

"It wasn't only about the treasure," he explained. "Not really. Not for myself, anyway. I am sick of the way these Anglo-Saxons hoard such wealth and keep it from us. I am sick of the way we feel like guests in this country, even when it has been agreed by law that we belong here too."

"So you poisoned your own men?!" exclaimed the

king.

"It was never going to kill them, just make them a little sick for a few days. I just wanted to give you a reason to attack these Anglo-Saxons, these Englishmen, these Christians." He was spitting the words in anger and hatred.

"You think it would have been a fair war?" asked the king. "Innocent people would have died. They would fight us back and perhaps even beat us! We

have a happy peace here now. We should cherish this peace. Just because we are different and worship different gods, that does not mean we should hate each other."

Max still didn't understand. "If it wasn't about the treasure, why did you hide the gold on the ship and not bury it?"

Olav gave a little smile. "I said it wasn't ONLY about the treasure. I wasn't going to waste those riches by burying them in the ground! What use

would they be there?!"

With that, the king signalled to the guards to take the prisoner away.

"You are a traitor, so your punishment is exile," said the king. "You must leave our land and never return."

"But where can I go?" cried Olav.

The king smiled. "You must leave the Danelaw. There is only one place you can go."

Olav was desperately shaking his head. "No... No... NO! You can't make me live with THEM... With the Anglo-Saxons!"

The king was still smiling. "Actually, I think it is the most fitting punishment for your crime! Don't worry, Olav. I'm sure you will grow to love them with time."

Olav protested as he was taken away, but soon he was gone.

18

The King reached out a hand to Sigurd.

"I am very sorry that we doubted you," said the king. "Please accept my deepest apologies."

Sigurd bowed to his king and smiled. "Of course. I am very pleased we found the real thief."

The crowd was starting to leave and go back to their daily business, but there was one more thing the king had to do.

The king strolled outside the castle gates with Max, Katie and Eirik. They walked through the village and waited in the evening sunshine for Sigurd to bring Father Godwin.

When they arrived, the king spoke kindly to Father Godwin.

"Please accept my sincerest apologies for the way you have been treated," he said. "I am very embarrassed by Olav's actions and I hope you can forgive us. We're not all big brutes with a thirst for war."

With this, the king gave Father Godwin his chest full of golden crosses back.

Father Godwin smiled. "Of course I forgive you."

"Before we take you home to your monastery, I hope you will join us for a Viking tradition. One of our elders passed away yesterday, so we shall hold his funeral tonight."

Father Godwin's face became very serious. "Oh, I

am very sorry for your loss."

"Oh, no need for sorrow," replied the king happily. "He led a long and happy life. Tonight we celebrate his life and remember his laughter."

19

As night fell, everyone gathered together by the river, where the deceased man's body was placed onto his own longship. His weapons were placed alongside him and the ship was set alight.

Max and Katie watched with amazement as the fire quickly grew and spread, until the whole ship was ablaze. Sparks crackled and rained down like fireworks as people sang happy tunes together.

Max and Katie said goodbye to Eirik and wished him well, then stepped back into the shadows. Everyone was facing the burning ship, so Max and Katie's departure was unnoticed.

Katie could still feel the warmth of the fire on her face as they travelled back through time. They landed back in Max's bedroom feeling pleased that they had helped prevent an unnecessary war.

"The king was surprisingly kind to Olav," said

Katie. "Most kings in history would have sentenced a traitor to death."

Max nodded. "You're right," he agreed. "But sending someone into exile can be just as awful. He is allowed to be hunted by the other Vikings. But even without that fear, it must be an empty, lonely life sometimes."

Katie frowned. "But he wasn't exiled in the middle of nowhere. There were lots of villages, towns and farms nearby. He wouldn't get lonely."

"No," said Max with a smile. "But for someone who hates Anglo-Saxons, it would be pretty uncomfortable at first!"

Katie laughed. "Maybe he'll change his mind and realise that people are people."

"I hope so," smiled Max.

See you on our next adventure!

Also in the Mysteries in Time series: